Carson-Dellosa Publishing LLC
P.O. Box 35665
Greensboro, NC 27425 USA

Library of Congress Cataloging-in-Publication Data is on file with the publisher.

Printed in China. All rights reserved.   ISBN 978-1-62399-170-8

01-092133753

THE Giant™
MAKES THE TEAM

Written by Linda Koons
Illustrated by Jennifer Harney

The Giant stared at the pink clock on the wall. *Good, just a few more minutes until Alex gets home*, he thought.

Audrey held up another card. "Who can tell me this word?" she asked in her best teacher voice.

"Dog, D-O-G," the Giant answered, which made Oliver perk up from his spot on the floor.

"Excellent!" Audrey said, nodding her head in approval.

But before Audrey could continue with the lesson, Alex burst into the room.

"Come on," he said, grabbing the Giant by the arm. "You're coming with me!"

Alex and the Giant took off for the baseball field where Alex's friends had already started a game.

"Why don't you try being the pitcher?" one of the boys said to the Giant after sizing him up. "Just throw the ball over home plate."

The Giant's first pitch was a strike.

"Yesssss!" he sang out, doing a little dance on the mound.

But after that, he could not get the ball anywhere near the plate.

"Why don't you try playing in the outfield?" Alex suggested.

The Giant stood in the outfield for several innings. Not a single ball came near him until finally there was a loud crack of the bat, and the ball shot up into the air.

"I've got it, I've got it," the Giant shouted as he ran back and forth so he was positioned right under the ball.

All the players were on their feet cheering as they watched the ball smack right into the Giant's big open hand…and then fall softly to the ground.

"That's OK," said Alex. "Maybe you'll like batting."

"Hey, batter batter!" chanted the kids on the sidelines as the Giant stepped into the box for his turn at bat.

The Giant tapped the ground with his bat and practiced his swing.

The pitcher wound up and threw his best pitch.

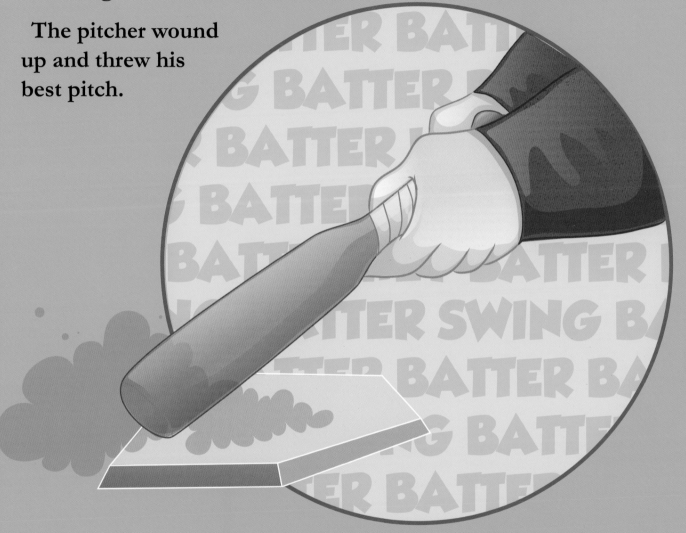

CRACK!

It was a hit! A big hit! A hit hard enough to tear apart the baseball and send the bat flying through the air in pieces.

"Duck!" the catcher yelled.

The pitcher jumped out of the way just in time.

After the close call with the bat, everyone decided to go home. "I guess baseball just isn't for me," said the Giant with disappointment.

That night after dinner, the Giant had the chance to try another sport when Alex and Audrey invited him to Family Bowling.

Audrey explained the game to the Giant while the Giant helped Audrey tie her bowling shoes.

This looks like fun, thought the Giant, as he watched the big, colorful balls rolling down the lanes. "Let's bowl!"

On Alex's turn, he knocked down all but two of the pins, and on Audrey's turn, she knocked down all ten on the first try.

When it was his turn, the Giant walked up to the line, looked down the long strip of shiny wood, and swung his arm around, making several loops in the air.

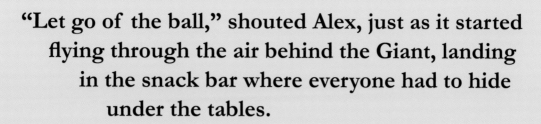

"Let go of the ball," shouted Alex, just as it started flying through the air behind the Giant, landing in the snack bar where everyone had to hide under the tables.

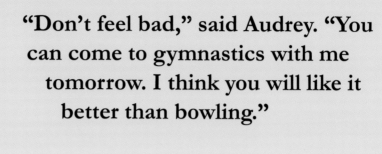

"Don't feel bad," said Audrey. "You can come to gymnastics with me tomorrow. I think you will like it better than bowling."

The next day, the Giant put on a very silly looking outfit and headed off to the gym. Audrey's friends were already there stretching and doing flips on the mats.

"Why don't you start on the balance beam?" Audrey suggested. "Watch me first."

Audrey climbed onto the beam and walked from one end to the other. At the end, she jumped off and threw her arms into the air.

"That doesn't look too hard," the Giant said.

But when he stepped onto the beam, it started to bend and shake before it completely buckled, sending the Giant crashing to the ground.

"That's OK. Let's try the mat," said Alex.

"I'll be your tumbling coach," Alex said. "We'll start with a basic somersault. Audrey, show the Giant what to do."

Audrey did several perfect somersaults, one after another.

"Ta-Da!" she said.

"Clear the mat," the Giant called out to everyone. "This is going to be the best somersault ever!"

The Giant tried to imitate Audrey, but after the first turn, he kept rolling and rolling.

When it looked like he was going to roll over Audrey and her friends, the Giant rolled straight into the wall.

"Are you okay?" Alex asked as he helped the Giant back onto his feet.

"Just a little dizzy from all the rolling," said the Giant, sounding a bit down.

"Hey, don't worry," replied Alex. "There are lots of sports left for you to try. I made a list."

The Giant and Alex
spent the rest of the day
trying almost every sport
on the list.

But nothing was quite right.

The next day at breakfast, the Giant barely touched his waffle even though Audrey made a smiley face with the syrup.

"What have you got there?" Alex said to Oliver when he came into the kitchen with a piece of paper in his mouth.

Alex looked at the paper and then pushed the plate with the waffle in front of the Giant. "Eat up, champ!" he exclaimed. "Football tryouts start today."

When they arrived at the football field, the Giant noticed the other players were almost as big as he was.

On the first play, the Giant tackled the runner from the other team. As he fell to the ground, the ball popped out of the runner's hands and right into the hands of the Giant. His teammates gave him high-fives all around.

When the Giant's team had the ball, someone handed it to him and he ran straight down the long field and into the end zone.

"Touchdown!" Alex yelled.

After awhile, the Giant decided he liked scoring touchdowns, but he didn't like crashing into other players and tackling them to the ground. It was like rolling into the wall at the gym.

Finally, a time out was called.

The Giant took off his helmet and carefully placed it on the bench next to where he and Alex were sitting.

"That's enough football for me," he said. "Let's go home."

GO GIANT!

At home, Audrey was in the yard throwing a tennis ball to Oliver. Oliver ran back and forth over and over again until he eventually got tired and laid down to watch the cars go by.

Usually the Giant loved watching Oliver play, but today it made him feel sad. *Even Oliver has a favorite sport!* he thought.

That night, the Giant was quiet at dinner. He barely touched his spaghetti.

"But pasghetti is your favorite!" Audrey said, trying to cheer him up.

"And we gave you extra meatballs!" added Alex.

"I don't want to see any kind of ball right now," said the Giant, "including a meatball. You can give my meatballs to Oliver."

Alex was worried the Giant was giving up with only one sport left to try.

Maybe we saved the best for last, thought Alex hopefully, as he looked down to the bottom of the paper.

When he saw what was written on the very last line, Alex broke into a big smile. "This is the one!" he shouted, as he rushed off to find the Giant.

And it was!

The Giant loved playing soccer!

He loved juggling the ball with his feet.

He loved passing the ball to his teammates.

His favorite part of all was blocking the goal.

"You are the best goalie we've ever had," said the captain.

The rest of soccer practice flew by learning drills and the rules of the game. When practice was over, everyone headed off the field in a big group.

The Giant stayed behind and crossed over to the team bench where Alex was busy packing up soccer balls.

"Hey, Alex," the Giant started. "I just wanted to say…"

But instead of finishing, the Giant scooped Alex up off the ground and wrapped his friend in a big thank-you hug.

"You're welcome," Alex said. "Congratulations, you made the team!"

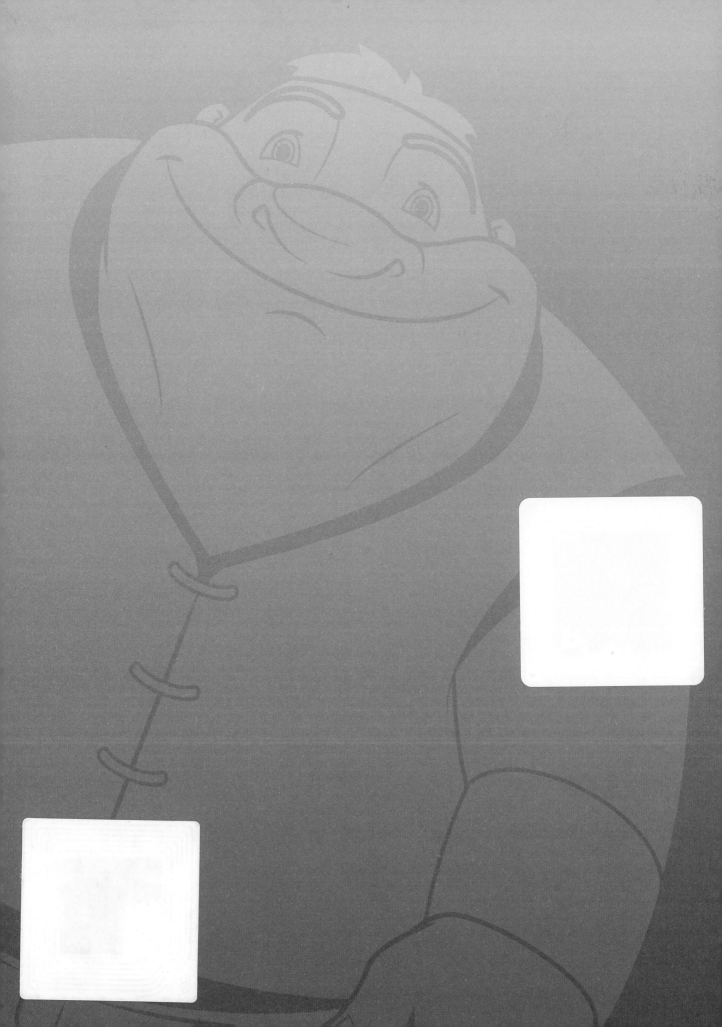